Why the Banana Split

Rick Walton

ILLUSTRATIONS BY Jimmy Holder

Gibbs Smith, Publisher
Salt Lake City

09 08 07 06 05 5 4 3 2 1

Published by
Gibbs Smith, Publisher
P.O. Box 667
Layton, Utah 84041

Book design by Trina Stahl

Printed and bound in China

Library of Congress Cataloging-in-Publication Data

Walton, Rick.
Why the banana split / Rich Walton; illustrated by Jimmy Holder.

— 1st ed.

p. cm.

Summary: The people and objects of a town panic and flee
when they see a Tyrannosaurus rex approaching, but they discover that only the bananas
have anything to fear from this fruit-eating dinosaur.

ISBN 0-87905-853-6 (hb)   ISBN 1-58685-841-6 (pb)
[Tyrannosaurus rex-Fiction. 2. Dinosaurs- Fiction.]
1. Holder, Jimmy, ill. 11. Title.
PZ7.W1774Wh 1998

[E]-dc21   98-5499

CIP
AC

To Rebecca and Brent Lloyd, who have taken off.
We're looking forward to their return.

—R.W.

To Robert Holder and Betty Brundick,
for sending me to art school.

—J. H.

When Rex came to town, everyone looked at his huge head high in the air and at his large sharp teeth.

And they screamed. "DINOSAUR!
DINOSAUR! RUN AWAY! RUN AWAY!"
And they did.

The jump ropes skipped town,

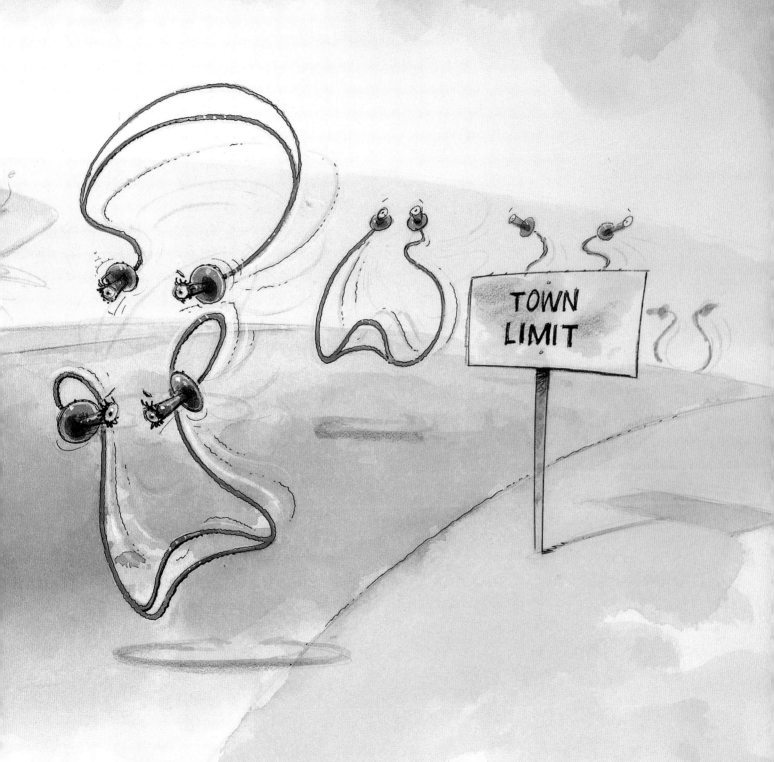

and the astronauts took off.

The bananas split, peeled out, slipped away.

The frogs hopped a train,
and that train made tracks.

The basketball players went traveling,

while the baseball players struck out on their own.

"Good buy," said the shoppers.
"Buy buy," said the shopkeepers.

The jackhammers hit the road.
The lettuce headed out.

The trees took their leaves.
The water ran off.

The boots took a hike,
and the knives cut and ran.

The snakes said, "Sso long,"
and the cows mooved on.

"Why are you all running away?" asked Rex.

"If you're coming, we're going," said the drum, just as he was ready to beat it. "We don't want you to eat us."

"But I only eat fruit!" said Rex.

"Really?" said the drum. "In that case, HEY, EVERYONE! COME ON BACK!"

And they did.

All except for the bananas.